Disney
PRINCESS

My Princess Collection

Dot

The Littlest Princess

Book Ten

BASED ON THE Disney · PIXAR FILM *A Bug's Life*

Written by M. L. Dunham

For information address Disney Press, 114 Fifth Avenue,
New York, New York 10011-5690.
Printed in China
First Edition
5 7 9 10 8 6 4
ISBN 0-7868-4603-8

For more Disney Press fun,
visit www.disneybooks.com

Chapter One

Hi, there. My name's Dot. Actually, I'm Princess Dot, next in line to be queen of the whole anthill! Of course, my sister, Atta, is actually queen now, so I'll most likely be a princess for a long time.

Don't get me wrong—I like being a princess, but to be honest with you, I'd rather play around and be a member of my Blueberry troop than perform royal duties. And besides, Atta is a good queen even though she worries a lot.

However, she's a whole lot better than she used to be, I'll tell you that much. When she was a queen-in-training, she used to freak out over everything. Of course, there used to be a lot to freak out about. . . .

Chapter Two

You see, our anthill used to be in a ton of trouble. There were these big, mean old grasshoppers who would come to collect most of the grain we harvested every year. We were all terrified of those grasshoppers. They barely left us enough food for ourselves for the winter.

Poor Atta— I have to admit she was stepping up to the throne at a bad time.

Now, my friend Flik—he's a really cool guy. He's an inventor, and let me tell you, he can invent anything! Once, he made a telescope out of a drop of water that he put inside a rolled-up leaf!

Anyway, during the last harvest we ever did for the grasshoppers, Flik invented a harvesting machine. It was really cool, but nobody except me would listen to him and see what amazing things his machine could do. Maybe if they had, things would have been different.

Chapter Three

One day, we heard the grasshoppers arriving, so we all ran inside the anthill. Flik was left outside with his invention. Now, I told you Flik was cool. But what I didn't tell you was that he could be kind of clumsy, too. He ended up knocking the entire offering of grain over the ledge and into the river below!

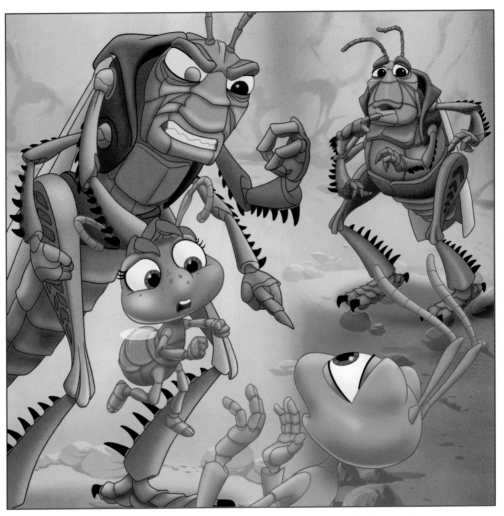

Now, we were in awfully big trouble! The grasshoppers got really mad, and one of them even picked me up and threatened to squish me! *Eek!* That's an ant's worst nightmare!

Flik felt so bad that he came up with a plan to make things better. He decided to leave our island to go out in search of warrior bugs to protect us. No ant had ever left Ant Island before.

"Good luck, Flik!" I shouted as he flew away on a dandelion puff.

Nobody believed he could do it—nobody except me, that is.

"You just watch," I said. "He'll get the bestest, roughest bugs you've ever seen!"

And guess what? He did! Well, sort of.

The only problem was that the warrior bugs
Flik brought back were actually circus bugs. It
was a tiny mistake, but it could still work out.
At least, I *thought* it could.

Chapter Four

Flik got the circus bugs and me and my whole Blueberry troop to help him with his plan. We made a giant fake bird out of leaves and twigs. So when the grasshoppers returned to get their food, we would scare them by crawling inside the bird and flying it right at them. It was a daring plan and Flik was great. He was like the captain of our ship.

"Blueberries ready?" he asked us when we were loaded inside the bird.

"Ready!" we shouted back.

Then—*whoosh!*—we were flying! And we really scared those mean old grasshoppers. They thought they were going to get eaten by our bird! But then we kind of crashed. None of us got hurt, but the grasshoppers figured out what was going on. They realized we weren't a real bird, after all.

But Flik was really brave. He had stood up to the grasshoppers and got the whole colony to follow him!

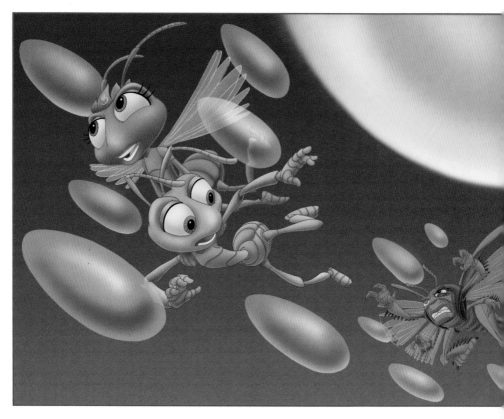

And Atta helped him, too. Together, they fought off the biggest, meanest grasshopper of all! It was so cool!

In the end, those mean old grasshoppers were scared away for good—especially after a real, live bird chased them down!

Chapter Five

In the end, the only sad part was that the circus bugs had to leave. P.T. Flea, the owner of the circus, asked Flik to join them, too.

"Sure you can't tour with us?" he asked.

But Flik just said, "Sorry. My place is here."

Anyway, the circus bugs all promised to come back and visit us at our little anthill. I sure hope they do.

In the meantime, I think Atta has a crush on Flik. I mean, it's always been totally obvious that *he* had a crush on her, but this is the first time I've seen her let him hold her hand and stuff. It's kind of gross, but I guess if I have to have a brother-in-law, Flik would be my first choice.

Anyway, I've got to go now. I want to
practice my flying before supper. See ya later!